P9-EGC-762

RAGGEDY ANN AND ANDY AND THE NICE FAT POLICEMAN

WORTH GRUELLE

RAGGEDY ANN and ANDY and the NICE FAT POLICEMAN

by JOHNNY GRUELLE

THE BOBBS-MERRILL COMPANY, INC.
A SUBSIDIARY OF HOWARD W. SAMS & CO., INC.
Publishers • INDIANAPOLIS • NEW YORK

1960

PRINTED IN THE UNITED STATES OF AMERICA

To Caroline

WORTH GRUELLE

Chapter One

IT WAS a lovely day in June. The birds were singing, the bees were buzzing and the air was filled with perfume of the flowers. Raggedy Ann and Raggedy Andy just could not stay another minute in the nursery where Marcella left them when she kissed them goodby very early that morning and hurried away with mother for a day of shopping in town.

Raggedy Andy took Raggedy Ann's hand and they both slid quietly from the little chair.

"Where are we going?" asked Raggedy Ann.

"To the Deep Woods in search of adventure!" replied Raggedy Andy, as they scampered down the stairs.

They had to be careful for Dinah, the cook, was in the kitchen and it would never do for her to see them.

In another minute both dolls were racing through the buttercups and daisies as they crossed the Golden Meadow on the way to the Deep, Deep Woods.

They found a tiny path into the Woods which they had not known before.

"We have never taken this path, Raggedy Andy!" said Raggedy Ann as she looked around. "Maybe we will get lost!"

"Oh, Raggedy Ann, you know the gnomes and fairies and the little woodland creatures will show us the way home!" Raggedy Andy assured her as he took her hand and they gaily skipped down the cool, green path.

They had gone but a little way, when, at a turn in the path, they came to a pretty little white house. It had green shutters and a red roof and was in a clearing where the sunlight streamed in and pretty flowers were growing all about the lovely little yard.

"Listen!" Raggedy Ann said, as they both stopped suddenly, "Someone is crying!"

"Shall we go in and see if we can be of help?" asked Raggedy Andy.

"My goodness, yes!" Raggedy Ann replied as she led the way inside.

"Why, it's a Nice Fat Policeman crying!" Raggedy Ann whispered.

The two dolls stood silently and waited until the Policeman looked up. When he saw them, he burst out crying louder than ever. Raggedy Ann went over and tried to comfort him as she wiped his tears away with her pocket hanky.

"Mercy me!" Raggedy Ann laughed, although she felt a lump in her cotton-stuffed throat, "Why are you crying so, Mister Policeman?"

"Oh, it is just too sad, Raggedy Ann and Raggedy Andy!" the Policeman replied between sobs, "I have to arrest Mr. Hooligooly!"

The Raggedys never had heard of Mr. Hooligooly, but they felt sad just the same.

"And," the Policeman wailed, "I have never, never arrested anyone and it makes me feel so unhappy, I shall never be able to do it!"

"Shucks!" Raggedy Andy said, "What has Mr. Hooligooly done, Mr. Policeman?"

"I really do not know!" the Policeman replied, "I found a note pinned to my front door which said, PLEASE ARREST MR. HOOLIGOOLY!"

"Perhaps someone is angry with Mr. Hooligooly and would like to get him into trouble," Raggedy Ann thought out loud. "Mr. Hooligooly may not have done anything wrong, at all."

"That is quite true, Raggedy Ann!" the Policeman said as a smile came to his face and Raggedy Ann dried the last of his tears. "Let us go and see Mr. Hooligooly!"

The Policeman put on his policeman's hat and the Raggedys went with him to Mr. Hooligooly's house which was just at the next bend in the path through the Deep Woods.

When they reached the front steps of the Hooligooly house, the Policeman caught Raggedy Ann's arm and said, "I do not want to arrest Mr. Hooligooly today. Let us go back to my house!"

"But, Mister Policeman!" Raggedy Ann said with surprise, "You came here to see Mr. Hooligooly to try and find out who wrote the note asking you to arrest him!"

"Hmmm, that is quite true, Raggedy Ann!" the Policeman replied, "Still, I think I had better run home and see if the fire has gone out!"

"But you did not have a fire in the stove, I am sure!" Raggedy Ann said.

"Anyway, I do not believe Mr. Hooligooly is at home!" said the Nice Policeman.

"We will knock at the door and soon see!" Raggedy Andy suggested.

"Oh, dear!" the Nice Fat Policeman sighed, "I wish I had not come. I feel something dreadful is about to happen!"

Raggedy Andy wiggled his shoe button eye at Raggedy Ann, that was his way of winking.

"I'll knock at the door!" said Raggedy Andy as he moved in that direction.

The Policeman took Raggedy Ann by the arm. "Raggedy Ann!" he said, "You and I will hide behind this tree so that I can easily arrest Mr. Hooligooly if he is unpleasant to Raggedy Andy!"

Raggedy Ann helped the Nice Fat Policeman to hide. For, the Policeman felt so sad at the thought of having to arrest Mr. Hooligooly, that his knees knocked together and his teeth chattered and tears came into his kindly eyes.

Raggedy Andy went up to the front door and knocked softly. There was no answer.

"Goody!" the Nice Policeman cried, "He is not at home!"

Raggedy Andy knocked again and this time rather loudly.

"Oh, dear me!" the Policeman sighed. "Do not knock so loudly, Raggedy Andy. You may wake him up—I mean, Mr. Hooligooly is not at home, so let us go back to my house!"

However, Raggedy Andy knew Mr. Hooligooly was at home for he could hear someone moving about inside.

Raggedy Andy knocked again ever so loudly, KNOCK! KNOCK!

"Who's there?" Mr. Hooligooly called.

"There, you see! Oh, now you have done it!" the Nice Policeman wailed. And he would have run home if Raggedy Ann had not held to his coat tails.

"The Nice Fat Policeman came to arrest you!" Raggedy Ann called to Mr. Hooligooly. "He is hiding behind the tree over there!"

Mr. Hooligooly stuck his head out of the door and looked around. "Will you all come right in and meet Mrs. Hooligooly?" he invited politely.

"Thank you!" said Raggedy Andy as he stepped inside and Raggedy Ann came from behind the tree almost dragging the Nice Fat Policeman.

After the proper introductions, Mr. Hooligooly looked

right at the Nice Policeman and said with a smile, "So you came to arrest me, did you?"

"Oh, yes!" the Policeman replied as though he had forgotten. "That was what I came for but I am in no hurry about it."

Raggedy Ann liked Mr. and Mrs. Hooligooly from the minute she saw them. They both had such cheery smiles and merry twinkles in their eyes.

Mrs. Hooligooly brought in some lemonade and cookies which she had just made and it seemed as though they were having a party.

"I am glad, Mister Policeman, you are in no hurry to arrest me!" Mr. Hooligooly said with a chuckle and Raggedy Ann was sure she saw him wink his eye.

"I am glad, too!" the Nice Policeman said, "For, whenever I arrest anyone, I arrest him, that's what. Sometimes I just take him by the collar and hustle him right down to the police station so fast he does not know what's happening. You know, I just hid behind that tree so that I could arrest you if you tried to harm Raggedy Andy!"

Mr. Hooligooly scratched his head as though something funny amused him. "I never will forget the night six

enormous, fat policemen tried to arrest me and I fastened each of them to a tree with his very own belt and they never came back to bother me."

The Nice Fat Policeman choked on the piece of cookie he was eating as he got up quickly from his chair. "I just happened to think!" he gasped between chokes, "I didn't put the cat out and he may eat the canary bird. I must hurry home!"

Mrs. Hooligooly caught the Policeman's arm as he started for the door. "Don't you pay any attention to Harry Hooligooly!" she said, "He is always joking. What he meant was that he dreamed six enormous, fat policemen tried to arrest him. He was snoring so loudly that I poked him and woke him up or the policemen would surely have arrested him."

"I must hurry!" the Nice Policeman said, "By this time the canary bird has more than likely eaten the cat!"

And he would have gone if Mr. Hooligooly had not taken the Policeman's other arm and helped Mrs. Hooligooly drag him back to his chair.

"Now, Mister Policeman, just make yourself comfortable," Mrs. Hooligooly said as she passed him the cookies and lemonade, "and I am sure Harry Hooligooly will let you arrest him presently!"

"Sure you may arrest me!" said Harry Hooligooly. He always wanted to be helpful.

"I shall not arrest you!" the Nice Policeman said. "Why should I? Have you done anything wrong?"

"I am sure he has done nothing wrong!" answered Mrs. Hooligooly. "Harry is just the kindest person you ever saw."

"Then we must find the one who wrote the note asking me to arrest you, so that I may arrest him," said the Policeman.

"We know who wrote the note and pinned it on your front door," Mrs. Hooligooly told the Policeman, "and when you have finished your lemonade we will tell you the whole story."

"I am through now, so please tell us," begged the Nice Policeman.

"I will tell you the story," Mrs. Hooligooly continued, "but, I shall not tell the name of the person, for I do not want to be a tattle-tale!"

"You are quite right!" the Nice Policeman agreed. "I would rather you did not tell us the name for that makes it

kind of a riddle. And, if I unriddle riddles, I will soon be promoted to be a detective."

"Well," Mrs. Hooligooly began, "quite a long time ago when Harry Hooligooly would go into the woods to gather sticks for firewood, he would often meet a queer little old man who would follow Harry all about.

"One evening when Harry Hooligooly came home with his bundle of sticks, the strange man was behind him and followed him into the house. We asked him to stay for supper but he shook his head and said, 'I lost a valuable stick in the woods and I believe Mr. Hooligooly found it!'

" 'If I did, it has been burned up!' Harry told him.

" 'No it hasn't!' the queer little man said, 'for, this stick cannot be burned up. It is a magic stick. It burns when you tell it to burn and goes out when you tell it to go out and the stick always stays the same. It never burns to ashes.'

" 'Does it belong to you?' I asked the strange man.

" 'No!' he said and then quickly corrected himself, 'I mean, yes it does!'

"So we knew the magic stick did not really belong to him.

"After that, Harry looked carefully every day for the magic stick and finally found it and we have it right here now. It is really wonderful. It burns when you wish it to burn and goes out as soon as you are finished cooking.

"The queer little man is sure we have the magic stick and that is why he wrote the note asking you to arrest Harry Hooligooly. He thinks that when Harry is locked up, he will come in and get the stick without any trouble."

"Hmmm!" the Nice Fat Policeman mused and then declared, "possession is nine points of the law and the Magic Stick is Harry Hooligooly's property. If the strange man bothers you again, you just call me and I will arrest him in a jiffy!"

"Thank you, Mister Policeman. You are very kind!" said Mrs. Hooligooly. "And now, if you boys will just visit awhile, Raggedy Ann and I will go to the kitchen and get dinner ready."

Mrs. Hooligooly took Raggedy Ann by the hand and they danced laughingly out to the kitchen to cook dinner with the Magic Stick.

It seemed but a little while when Raggedy Ann came into the room where Raggedy Andy and the Nice Policeman and Mr. Hooligooly were talking. "Mrs. Hooligooly has cooked the loveliest dinner over the Magic Burning Stick!" she said. "You should see how the Magic Stick works, Raggedy Andy!"

"I would like to!" Raggedy Andy replied.

"So would I!" the Nice Policeman added.

So Raggedy Ann took them out to the kitchen and showed them the Magic Burning Stick and how it worked.

Mrs. Hooligooly was just finishing the cooking and was making nice brown gravy.

When she wished the Stick to blaze real high, she said, "Please burn a little hotter, Magical Burning Stick!" And it was just like cooking with gas. The Magic Stick blazed higher until it reached just the right heat.

When Mrs. Hooligooly had finished the gravy, she said, "Now, go out, Magic Burning Stick!" and the blaze went out and the stick cooled.

"Now, Harry Hooligooly, please show the Nice Policeman and Raggedy Andy where they go to wash their hands and faces, and hurry for dinner will be on the table!"

"And be sure to wash your neck and ears, Harry!" Mrs. Hooligooly added as the three boys left the room.

Raggedy Ann was just placing the last chair at the

table when the three returned with faces shiny and bright from the good scrubbing.

Mrs. Hooligooly had roasted a nice turkey with dressing and had made cranberry sauce and fluffy mashed potatoes and gravy and mince pie.

"YUM, YUM!" the Nice Policeman said as he sat down to the table, "this is just like Thanksgiving and Christmas. Isn't it, Raggedy Andy?"

"Ooh, you bet it is!" Raggedy Andy agreed.

When they were all seated, Mrs. Hooligooly said, "Raggedy Ann, will you please ask the blessing?"

They all bowed their heads while Raggedy Ann said quietly,

"Lord, bless this meat that we shall eat,
This bread that we shall break,
Make all our actions kind and sweet,
We ask for Jesus sake. Amen!"

"We have a nice dinner like this every day, Mr. Policeman!" Harry Hooligooly said.

"Is that so?" the Policeman laughed, "Then I think I shall move right over and live here for I am very, very fond

of such delicious food!"

"We will be very happy to have you live with us!" Mr. and Mrs. Hooligooly both said.

"But," Mrs. Hooligooly added, "what will you do with the Police Station?"

"Oh, it can stay right where it is!" the Nice Policeman replied. "You see! I never have any prisoners anyway, so I can live here with you just as well as not. I'm tired of having nothing but pancakes every day!"

"Then that is settled!" Mrs. Hooligooly said and you could see by the twinkle in her eye that she was very happy at the thought of doing something nice for others.

"Yes, indeed!" Harry Hooligooly said, "when we finish

dinner, Raggedy Andy and I will walk over to your house with you and help you move your things. We have an extra bedroom for you!"

"All I shall need will be my nightie!" the Nice Policeman said as he passed his plate for another helping of turkey and cranberry sauce.

They were having a grand time because they all had good appetites.

When they had finished, Raggedy Ann brought in the wash cloth and wiped the faces of Raggedy Andy and Harry Hooligooly and the Nice Policeman. They had been careless in eating the mince pie and it was smeared around their mouths, just like most boys on Thanksgiving and Christmas Day.

"Now we will run over to my house and get my nightie!" the Nice Policeman said, "For I shall be very happy to live with the Hooligoolys from now on."

"We will be back in a few minutes, Henrietta!" Harry Hooligooly said to his wife as he and Raggedy Andy and the Nice Policeman started out the door.

"I am so glad that I will live with you, Harry Hooligooly!" the Nice Fat Policeman chuckled. "You have such good things to eat and I shall get fatter and fatter and fatter, I guess."

"You had better not get too fat!" Harry laughed, "for you will not be able to arrest anyone if you cannot run and catch him!"

This made the Policeman laugh for he had never arrested anyone in his life.

"I will be very much pleased if I eat so much and get so fat that I cannot arrest anyone," the Nice Policeman said. "It always makes me feel sad to think that some day I may have to arrest someone. I wish everyone in the whole wide world would always be good so that no one would ever have to be arrested and punished!"

"That would certainly be nice," Harry Hooligooly agreed, "if people would just stop to think how much more fun it is being good than being naughty, they would always be good. For, punishment always follows naughtiness and punishment is not one bit of fun."

And so, laughing and talking, the three walked through the Deep Woods until they came to the Policeman's house.

"Dear me!" the Nice Policeman exclaimed as he went in the front door, "someone has been in here and scattered things all topsy turvy!"

Chapter Two

THE Nice Policeman and Raggedy Andy and Harry Hooligooly hurried through the house and reached the kitchen just in time to see a funny looking little man run out the back door.

"Aha!" Harry Hooligooly cried, "that is the old man who claimed my Magic Burning Stick. Let's catch him!"

And all three raced out the back door after the little old man.

The little man had a good start but they could see him in the distance ahead.

They ran and ran for what seemed to be a long time, but really wasn't, and they were getting closer to the queer little man all the time, when suddenly he turned from the path and dashed into the front door of a funny little house. The three boys arrived just as the little man slammed the door and bolted it after him.

"Well!" Harry Hooligooly puffed between breaths, "I have wanted to know where this funny old man lives and this must be the place!"

When they had rested for a minute or two, the Nice Fat Policeman said nervously, "S-s-s-omeone had b-b-b-etter knock at the d-d-d-oor!"

Raggedy Andy stepped up and knocked at the door.

"I know who it is!" the queer old man called from inside, "and you can just run along home for I will not let you in!"

"Then we'll huff and we'll puff and we'll blow your house in!" the Nice Fat Policeman cried and then he remembered this was from a story his mother read to him when he was a little boy. "I mean," he corrected himself, "if you do not open the door at once, we will break it down!"

"Ha, ha, ha!" the queer old man laughed. "Why don't you try to open the door yourself? You are a 'fraidy calf policeman, that's what!"

"Maybe we had better go!" the Policeman suggested.

"Nonsense!" exclaimed Raggedy Andy, "I shall climb up on the roof and go down the chimney just like Santa Claus does at Christmastime. Then I will unlock the door and let you in so you can arrest the queer little man for going in your house and scattering the furniture about."

Harry Hooligooly gave Raggedy Andy a boost up the

rainspout and then sat down on the grass beside the Policeman. They watched Raggedy Andy climb to the roof and disappear down the chimney.

"Pretty soon we should hear Raggedy Andy scuffling with the queer little man!" the Policeman suggested.

"I imagine so!" Harry Hooligooly agreed.

But, although they listened and listened, they could not hear a sound coming from inside the house.

"Maybe Raggedy Andy has caught the queer old man and is busy tying him so that he cannot wiggle and twist and scratch and bite!" the Nice Policeman thought out loud.

"Yes! that is probably the reason Raggedy Andy does not unlock the door and let us in!" Harry Hooligooly said rather sadly.

"While you watch here, I will run home and get some cookies!" the Nice Policeman suggested.

"Oh, no!" said Harry Hooligooly, "you must stay here so that you can see the scuffle, if the queer old man comes out!"

"But, if I should see you wrestling, you know that I would have to arrest you, Harry. For, I have to arrest anyone who wrestles or fights in the Deep Woods!"

"That is so!" Harry remembered. "But I will not touch the queer little man unless he starts to wrestle with me first. Then I will just defend myself and you will have to arrest him for starting the disturbance."

"Why don't you find out why Raggedy Andy doesn't open the door?" the Nice Policeman suggested.

"Good idea!" said Harry, as he tiptoed up and peeped in the keyhole. He came quickly back to the side of the Policeman.

"What do you think?" Harry Hooligooly asked and

without waiting for an answer, went on, "the queer old man has done just like the little pig in the story of 'The Three Little Pigs.' He hung a pot of water on a big hook in the fireplace so Raggedy Andy would fall in the water when he came down the chimney. But Raggedy Andy's waist got caught on the big hook and he is hanging so that he cannot wiggle loose! Isn't that sad?"

The Nice Fat Policeman thought so, for he cried as though his heart would break. He cried so hard and so long that Harry Hooligooly had time to run to the Policeman's house and bring back one of the Policeman's extra large hankys to dry his tears.

"I will certainly have to arrest the queer old man for catching Raggedy Andy on that pot hook!" the Nice Fat Policeman declared, "for I am certain it is against the law to catch anyone on a pot hook and to let him wiggle and twist and not be able to touch the floor with his feet."

"Yes, indeed!" Harry Hooligooly agreed, "but wasn't Raggedy Andy brave to climb down the queer old man's chimney, though?"

"He surely was brave, but it seems to have done no good," said the Policeman, "for, now who will unlock the

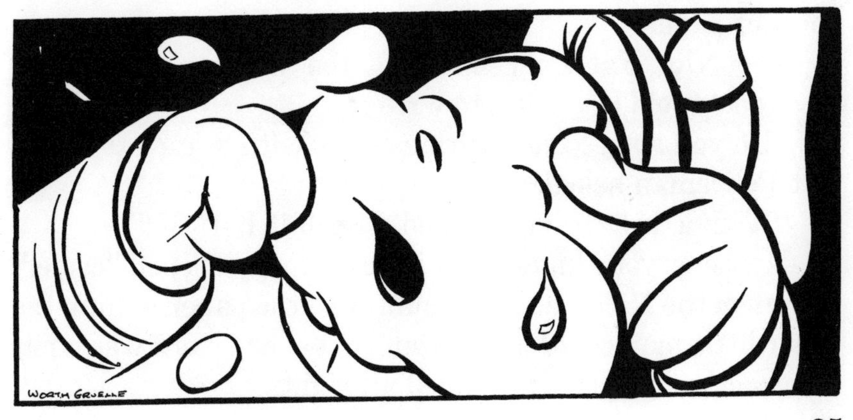

door so that I can get in the house to arrest the queer little man?"

"Perhaps if you would read one of those legal papers to him,—I think they are called 'warrants,'—and say, 'I have come to arrest you in the name of the Law,' the queer old man would be so frightened he would open the door. You could then arrest him while I take Raggedy Andy off the pot hook and brush the soot from his clothes and face."

"That is just what we will do!" the Policeman said. "I will run home and get a piece of paper and we will write out a warrant and I will read it to the queer little man."

So, Harry Hooligooly sat and watched the house while the Policeman ran home and brought back a pencil and sheet of paper.

The Nice Fat Policeman did the writing and Harry Hooligooly told him what to write.

"Do you spell 'come' with a 'k' or with a 'c'?" the Nice Fat Policeman asked.

"With a 'k'!" Harry replied, "Spell it K-U-M!"

Now everyone knows that is not the way to spell "come," but when the Nice Fat Policeman read the paper to him, the queer little man could not tell but that every word was written exactly right for it sounded all right.

After they had finished the writing and read it over to themselves, the Nice Fat Policeman walked bravely to the front door of the queer little man's house and knocked.

"Run home to your mama before I come out and give you a hard thump!" the queer little man called angrily.

"Do you see this paper?" the Nice Fat Policeman asked. But without waiting for the queer little man to reply, the policeman began to read it.

"I have come to arrest you in the name of the law. Open that door at once!"

"Ha, ha, haw!" the queer little man laughed, "just you tell me the name of the law, that's what I want to know! And I will open the door."

Inside the queer old man's house, Raggedy Andy still hung by his waist from the hook in the fireplace.

"If you knew how funny you looked, Raggedy Andy, with your face covered with soot and your rag legs wiggling, you would laugh at yourself!" the queer old man chuckled as he walked into the adjoining room.

Raggedy Andy made no reply for he knew it would do no good.

The queer old man was in the small room at the rear of

the house.

Raggedy Andy could not see him but could hear him chuckling to himself as though someone had told him a funny story.

Raggedy Andy heard the little old man open the back door very quietly and Raggedy Andy thought, now he will slip quietly out the back door and escape into the woods and Harry Hooligooly will come in and help me down from this hook.

But Raggedy Andy was mistaken.

The queer old man closed the back door and locked it. Then he ran into the room where Raggedy Andy was hanging from the hook, and peeped through the keyhole in the front door.

"I am playing a good joke on Harry Hooligooly and that Nice Fat Policeman," he said, as he winked slyly at Raggedy Andy. "I have made two magic pancakes and they will surely fool your friends. Just you wait and see!"

"I wish you would lift me from this pot hook, so that I can see, too!" Raggedy Andy said.

The queer little man went over to where Raggedy Andy was hanging and reached up as though to take him down. He stopped suddenly and said, "Indeed, I shall not take you

down, Raggedy Andy! If I do, you will wrestle with me and let the Fat Policeman and Harry Hooligooly come in!"

Raggedy Andy knew this was just what he had planned to do, so, again he remained silent.

"Ha, ha, ha, I thought so!" the queer old man chuckled. "The Fat Policeman has one magic pancake and Harry Hooligooly has the other. As soon as they eat the pancakes, they will both turn into little squealy pigs. Then I can go to the Hooligooly house and get the Magic Burning Stick. I wish they would hurry and eat the pancakes!"

Raggedy Andy felt badly at hearing this and being so that he could not help his friends, for, he did not want them changed into little squealy pigs.

Now Raggedy Andy knew for sure the queer little man was really a mean old magician.

When the queer little man had opened the back door and rolled out the magic pancakes, they kept right on rolling until one settled in the lap of the Nice Fat Policeman and the other in Harry Hooligooly's lap. Neither, of course, had any idea that the queer old man had made such delicious looking pancakes. Neither did they think of them as being magical pancakes for they looked just like all the other pancakes they had ever seen.

Harry Hooligooly and The Nice Fat Policeman wondered where the pancakes came from but they did not know that the queer little man was a magician and had rolled the pancakes out of his back door and told them to roll right into their laps.

"It is just dandy to have delicious pancakes roll right into our laps," the Policeman said, "and just when I was getting kind of hungry, too. Aren't you getting hungry, Harry?"

"I surely am!" Harry answered as he took a bite of the pancake.

The Nice Fat Policeman was just about to take a bite of

WORTH
GRUELLE

his pancake. He was looking right at Harry Hooligooly and Harry disappeared. The Policeman heard a squeal and at the exact spot where Harry had been, stood a little squealy pig.

"Dear me!" the Nice Fat Policeman cried in surprise as he threw his pancake away, "I shall not eat the pancake for it must surely be a magical one!"

The little squealy pig ran away into the bushes and the kind hearted Policeman sat down feeling very sad.

"I'll just bet the queer old man made those pancakes!" the Policeman said to himself. "I must think of some way to arrest him, now that I know he is so mean as to change kind Harry Hooligooly into a little squealy pig. The sooner I put him in jail the better, even if he does give me a hard thump and tweek my nose."

As he sat thinking very hard, the Nice Fat Policeman took a little blue book from his pocket. The book told how to be a detective and the Nice Policeman looked carefully to find a way to catch the queer old man and arrest him so that the Policeman could rescue Raggedy Andy and Harry Hooligooly.

"Ha, ha, Raggedy Andy!" the funny old Magician said as he turned from peeping through the keyhole, "Harry Hooligooly took a bite of my magic pancake, turned into a little squealy pig, and has run away into the woods."

"Now," he continued, "the Fat Policeman is going to eat his pancake and he will turn into a little squealy pig. Then I will hurry to the Hooligooly house and take the Magic Burning Stick!"

"You are a very mean person to change Harry Hooligooly into a squealy pig!" Raggedy Andy said. "How would you like to be changed into a pig and just go around wallowing in mud puddles?"

"What I want is the Magic Burning Stick!" the old Magician cried. "Then I can have a fire at any time to cook my magic potions and I will not have the bother of building one!"

The queer old man went again to the door and peeped through the keyhole. "I wonder why the Fat Policeman does not eat his pancake?" he said.

"I hope he doesn't take even one teeny weeny bite!" Raggedy Andy said.

This made the old magician very angry. He opened the door a little way and called to the Nice Fat Policeman who was sitting under a tree reading from a little blue book, "Why don't you eat your nice pancake?"

"Because, I am too busy reading how to become a detective. Then I will find a way to catch you and lock you up!"

the Policeman replied, "Besides, it is a magic pancake and will change me into a pig if I eat it, just as it did to Harry Hooligooly!"

"Silly!" the old magician laughed. "Don't you know that the magical pancake will make you the greatest detective ever? Just you take a bite and see! Then you will not need to read that little blue book."

"Honest, won't I have to read the little blue book if I eat the pancake?" the Nice Fat Policeman asked.

"Honest!" the old magician answered, "If you eat the pancake, you will not read the little blue book!"

"Then I shall eat the pancake!" the Policeman said, "But, remember, if you are telling me a story, I shall have to arrest you, sure pop!"

The Nice Fat Policeman found the pancake that he had thrown away in the bushes and took a bite.

"Ha, ha, ha!" the old magician shrieked as he kicked his heels in the air. "See him run! He turned into a nice little fat squealy pig. Whee! Now I can run over to Harry Hooligooly's house and get the Magic Burning Stick."

And so saying, the mean old Magician ran out the door and left Raggedy Andy hanging from the pot hook in the chimney.

Chapter Three

ALL this time, Raggedy Ann was at Mrs. Hooligooly's house helping her make lovely doughnuts and pies and cookies and cream puffs. Now they had finished and had put the house in order and made the beds and they began to wonder what could be keeping Harry Hooligooly and Raggedy Andy and the Nice Fat Policeman so long, when all they had to do was help the Policeman get his nightie and come right back.

"They should have been back a long time ago," Mrs. Hooligooly said, "I am beginning to feel worried. If they do not come in a few minutes, we had better go see what is keeping them!"

Raggedy Ann was just about to agree with Mrs. Hooligooly but before she could speak, a little squealy pig dressed in Harry Hooligooly's clothes came running into the house.

"Mercy me!" Mrs. Hooligooly cried, "What do you mean running into my nice clean house?" And, catching up the broom she was just about to give the little pig a whack, when Raggedy Ann cried, "Stop, Mrs. Hooligooly! That must be Harry Hooligooly and he has been changed into a little squealy pig!"

The little pig nodded his head to Raggedy Ann and to Mrs. Hooligooly as though he were trying to say, "Yes, that is true!"

Just then there was more squealing outside and right into the house came another little pig running and squealing. This was a fat little pig and was wearing the Policeman's clothes.

"Oh, dear!" Raggedy Ann cried, "The Policeman has been changed into a pig, too. And, I suppose Raggedy Andy will come running in squealing in another minute!"

But Raggedy Andy did not come, instead came the queer little old man.

Raggedy Ann quickly closed the doors and locked them. She took Mrs. Hooligooly's broom and waited near the front door to see what the queer little old man would do.

He went to the back door and knocked, but no one answered so he walked up on the front porch and, seeing a window partly open, stuck his head in to see if anyone was at home. Just then Raggedy Ann brought the broom down on the little old man's head with a THUMP.

"Oh, excuse me!" Raggedy Ann said, "Did I hit you on the head?"

"Yes, you did!" the Magician howled, "And it doesn't feel good either!"

"Then you should not come snooping and peeping in other people's windows. It isn't polite!" Raggedy Ann said as she closed the window and fastened the catch.

"If you do not open that door, I shall change you all into little squealy pigs!" the mean Magician howled.

"How did you change Harry Hooligooly and the Nice Fat Policeman into pigs?" Raggedy Ann asked.

"Ha, ha, ha!" the Magician laughed, "I made two magical pancakes and as soon as they took a bite, they changed into little pigs!"

Raggedy Ann did not say anything to Mrs. Hooligooly, but she saw a piece of the magical pancake sticking out of the pocket of one of the little pigs.

Raggedy Ann took this piece of pancake and Mrs. Hooligooly never noticed it.

Then Raggedy Ann broke the piece of pancake into tiny bits and mixed them into the filling of a nice large cream puff which she took with her to the front door.

"Will you change Harry Hooligooly and the Nice Policeman back to their own selves?" Raggedy Ann asked the Magician through the keyhole.

"Indeed I shall not unless you give me the Magic Burning Stick first!" the Magician replied.

"Oh, no!" Raggedy Ann said, "If we should give you the Burning Stick first, you would just run away and not change the pigs back into Harry Hooligooly and the Nice Fat Policeman."

"O very well, then if you will open the door and put the Magic Stick where I can see it, I will come in and change them back. Then you can give me the Magic Stick.

Raggedy Ann placed the cream puff on the table where the Magician would be sure to see it and then got the Burning Stick from the kitchen and put it in the corner. She went over and opened the door.

"Come in!" she said to the Magician, "Here are the two little pigs and you just turn them quickly back into the Policeman and Harry Hooligooly!"

The Magician looked carefully around the room and was glad to see the Magic Burning Stick in the corner.

"I must hold the Magic Stick!" he said as he took the stick in his hand. Then he noticed the lovely cream puff on the table. "Aha! what a delicious looking cream puff!" he remarked as he took it from the table without asking if he might have it.

"Do not eat that until you have changed the two little pigs back as you promised!" Raggedy Ann warned.

But the mean Magician laughed and walked out the door.

"Ha, ha, ha!" he cried, "That's the time I fooled you! Now I have the Magic Burning Stick, you can all whistle!" And he began to eat the cream puff.

He had taken just one bite when he turned quickly into a little fat squealy pig, the Magic Burning Stick dropped to the ground, and he scampered squealing through the woods to his house.

"There!" said Raggedy Ann as she picked up the Magic Stick and put it back in its place in the kitchen, "I gave him some of his own medicine and I'll bet he is sorry he ever made those magical pancakes!"

"I wish we could find a way to change these pigs back to

Harry and the Policeman!" Mrs. Hooligooly wished aloud. "I do not like to have pigs in my parlor even if they are my own. Then too, I am sure they do not enjoy being pigs!"

"I do not believe they do!" Raggedy Ann said. "Maybe if we go to the Magician's house, we can go inside and hunt through his books of magic and find out how to change these pigs back into Harry and the Policeman!"

"That is a splendid idea, Raggedy Ann!" Mrs. Hooligooly said, "Shall we take the two little pigs with us?"

"Do you want to go with us?" Raggedy Ann asked the two little pigs.

Both little pigs nodded their heads and squealed so loudly that Mrs. Hooligooly held her hands over her ears.

"They want to go!" Raggedy Ann laughed as she started out the door.

It did not take very long for them to reach the Magician's house and there on the front porch sat the Magician pig squealing ever and ever so loudly.

Raggedy Ann walked onto the porch and the mean Magician pig would have bitten her if the Nice Fat Policeman pig had not caught and held the Magician pig by the ear.

Raggedy Ann was surprised, when she looked inside to find Raggedy Andy hanging from the pot hook and she rushed over and helped him down. Mrs. Hooligooly helped Raggedy Ann brush the soot and ashes from Raggedy Andy's clothes and face and then they all started looking around.

They went into the little back room and found shelves covered with bottles of all sorts of magic potions and powders. On the table was the Magician's big red Book of Magic. Raggedy Ann and Andy lost no time in finding the place where it told how to change one thing to another and the proper magical medicine to use. They looked among the bottles and found the medicine.

Raggedy Ann called the two little pigs and sprinkled some of the magic medicine on them, then she read the magic words from the red book, and, lo and behold! there stood Harry Hooligooly and the Nice Fat Policeman just as good as ever.

"Wheee!" yelled Harry Hooligooly as soon as he found he was himself again, "I was afraid I would have to remain a little squealy pig for ever and ever!"

"So was I!" said the Nice Fat Policeman as he jumped around for joy.

Now Raggedy Ann, because she has a nice candy heart

and is so kind and thoughtful, called the little mean Magician pig in from the front porch and changed him back into the Magician himself.

"Just you wait!" the mean Magician said, "I shall soon change you all into something you do not like! You just better watch out!"

"You should be grateful to Raggedy Ann for changing you from a little squealy pig to your own self again!" Harry Hooligooly said.

"Is that so?" the mean creature howled. "I never would have been a squealy pig if it had not been for Raggedy Ann. I know that she put magic in that cream puff I ate!"

"You should not have eaten it!" Raggedy Ann said, "It did not belong to you and, when you take something that does not belong to you, you always get into trouble. Beside, if you had not made those terrible magic pancakes you would not have been changed to a pig! You brought every bit of trouble on yourself!"

"And," laughed Raggedy Ann, "That is always the way! Whenever you do an unkind thing to another, the unkindness always returns to the one who starts it and always hurts him much more!"

"Anyway, it is all your fault, Raggedy Ann!" the mean little old Magician howled. "Even if I did make the magic pancakes to change Harry Hooligooly and the Policeman into little pigs, you had no right to change me into a pig!"

"I didn't!" Raggedy Ann laughed, "You changed yourself by eating the cream puff which you took without asking if you might have it!"

"I don't care!" the Magician howled, "I shall make a lot of magic medicine and change every last one of you! You wait and see!"

"See here!" the Nice Fat Policeman said sternly, "You

must be careful how you talk to a lady. I may arrest you before you know it!"

At this the Magician laughed real loudly, like this—HAW, HAW, HAW! and he tweeked the Policeman's nose so hard, the Policeman had to cry right in Raggedy Ann's apron.

Raggedy Andy could not sit idly by and see a friend injured in this way. He made a flying tackle of the Magician and they both went down in a heap. They wrestled until the dust flew but Raggedy Andy finally put the Magician down and sat on him. By this time the Policeman's tears had changed to laughs as he cheered Raggedy Andy on and when the Magician had been put down, the Policeman arrested him and locked him in the jail.

Of course, Raggedy Ann and Raggedy Andy and Mr. and Mrs. Hooligooly went along and watched the Nice Fat Policeman put the mean old Magician in a cell with big iron doors.

"Just you wait!" the Magician howled through the bars of his cell, "When I get out, you'll be sorry. I shall make some more magic pancakes and change you all into pigs, for I intend to get the Magic Burning Stick from the Hooligoolys."

"Just you let me catch you doing that, and I'll arrest you again!" the Nice Fat Policeman promised.

"Now," the Policeman said as he turned to his friends, "I will get my nightie and we will all go back to the Hooligooly's house!"

"But, how can you leave the Magician a prisoner?" Raggedy Andy wanted to know. "Where is the judge?"

"Oh, the prisoner is all right!" the Policeman said, "Anyway, there isn't any judge so we will just let the Magician stay in prison for six weeks and that should cure him of his meanness!"

"Then we will have to get him some food!" Raggedy Ann said.

"Indeed!" the Magician screamed, "I would not eat any food you brought to me. I would be afraid that it was magic food and would change me into something I would not like to be. I will not eat a thing. I'll just stay here and starve and then you will be very sorry you treated me so terribly!"

"Aren't you silly?" Raggedy Ann said. "If you are put in prison and refuse to eat, it is you who are treating yourself badly!"

But the Magician only howled the louder and said it

would be their fault if he grew ever and ever so thin and hungry.

"What had we better do?" the Nice Fat Policeman asked, "We can't let the foolish creature starve, although it would be his own fault!"

"You may do just as you think best!" Raggedy Ann said, "But I believe he will be glad to have some food in a little while!"

"No sir. I shall not!" the Magician howled. "Oh!

You'll be sorry! You'll be sorry!"

The Nice Fat Policeman was confused by all the noise and hubbub. "Maybe I had better let him go if he will promise not to take the Magic Burning Stick from the Hooligoolys," he thought out loud.

"I shall not promise that!" the Magician said. "You must give me the Magic Stick first and then I will tell you what I shall do!"

"That is absolutely silly!" the Policeman said with disgust. "You can just stay in there six weeks and see how you like it."

The Policeman went to his room and came back with his nightie. "All right, everybody!" he said, "I am ready to go to live with the Hooligoolys!" And as they started out the door with the Magician howling away for dear life, the Policeman whispered to Raggedy Ann, "We will bring him some food very shortly!"

On the way through the quiet woods, Raggedy Ann said, "I do not see why people want to be mean and disagreeable. When a person is mean like the Magician, no one likes him and it causes the mean person no end of trouble!"

It was lunch time when our friends reached the house

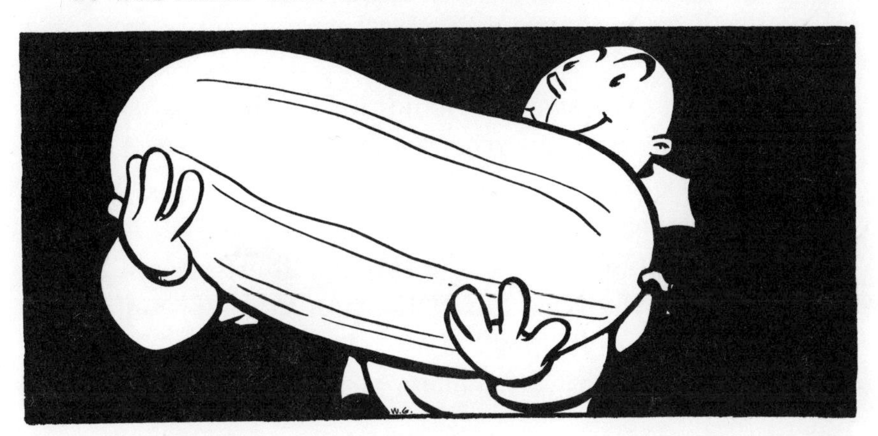

of the Hooligoolys and, while Raggedy Ann and Mrs. Hooligooly got things ready, Harry went to the garden and brought in a delicious watermelon and a basket full of ice cream cones picked fresh from the ice cream cone bushes growing there. There was a bush for each flavor,—vanilla, chocolate and strawberry, and the colors looked very pretty, —white and brown and pink.

As they finished the delicious luncheon, Raggedy Andy suggested that they show their friendliness and kindly hearts by taking a nice assortment of goodies over to the Magician.

"Oh, yes!" they all agreed. "Let's do!"

Raggedy Ann filled a large basket with all sorts of

goodies and she and the Nice Fat Policeman took it to the Policeman's home where the Magician was locked up.

"Guess what we have brought you, and we will give it to you!" Raggedy Ann said merrily to the Magician.

"Ha, I can guess that easily!" the Magician replied, "You have a basket filled with food, that's what. But you need not expect me to eat any of it!"

"Why, there are nice cookies and watermelon and ice cream cones and cream puffs!" Raggedy Ann said. "And Mrs. Hooligooly makes the nicest cream puffs you ever tasted!"

"I shall not eat even one smidgin!" yelled the Magician. "Do you think that I have forgotten that I tasted one of Mrs. Hooligooly's cream puffs and that it changed me into a little fat squealy pig? No sir!"

"I think Magicians are just the silliest people in the whole world!" the Nice Fat Policeman said, "I wouldn't be a magician for anything!"

"You unlock this cell door and let me go!" the Magician howled.

Raggedy Ann and the Policeman could just not keep from laughing and this made the mean Magician furious.

"We shall not stay if you are going to act that way, Mr.

Magician!" Raggedy Ann said, "We can have a great deal more fun at Harry Hooligooly's!"

So, Raggedy Ann put the basket of goodies where the Magician could reach them. She called good bye to him and hand in hand she and the Policeman skipped down the path that led to the Hooligooly's house.

As they went merrily along the path they passed a little puppy dog, but they did not see him for he hid in the bushes until they had passed and then dashed to the Policeman's house and in the door which was open.

"It's Hector!" the Magician cried with glee, when he saw the puppy dog. "I shall have Hector taste the goodies in the basket and see if he turns into anything."

When Hector had tried a little bit of everything in the basket and nothing happened to him, the mean old Magician hurried and ate everything himself and would not give one teeny weeny bite to good old Hector. There was so much and the Magician ate it in such a hurry that he got a terrible stomach ache. And it served the mean old creature just right for being so selfish and stingy with his faithful little dog.

The Magician sat on the floor of the prison cell in the Nice Policeman's house and howled and howled, while just outside the bars his puppy dog, Hector, jumped up and down and barked and barked.

Then, suddenly the Magician stopped crying, for his stomach ache had left. Hector stopped barking as the Magician turned to him and said, "I wish you would run home, Hector, and bring me my Book of Magic. It is on the table in the parlor!"

The Magician was hardly through speaking when Hector dashed out the door and was on his way. In no time at all the little puppy dog was back carrying the book in his mouth, and it was a heavy book, too.

"Ah, good old Hector!" exclaimed the Magician as he reached through the bars and picked up the Book of Magic with one hand and with the other gave the obedient puppy dog a loving pat, "The Book will soon tell me how to escape from this miserable prison."

The Magician thought first of changing himself to a mouse and then he could easily go out between the bars of the cell. But, he happened to think, "No! that will never do. Hector will not know the mouse is his master and he might catch me and eat me. Then I would be in a fine fix. No, that will never do!"

Then he thought he would change himself into a cat and

squeeze easily between the bars of the cell. And he had almost said the Magic words to make the change, when he thought, "No! if I do that, Hector will chase me up a tree. I must think of something else!"

The Magician puzzled his brain to think of some kind of animal to change himself to so that he could escape from prison. He was almost to the point of giving up when the idea came to him. "If I can make myself real thin, as thin as a lath almost, then I can walk right between the bars and be out in a jiffy!"

The Magician found the place in the Book of Magic that told just how to do this, and before Hector could wag his tail three times, the Magician was out of the cell and on his way through the woods.

As soon as he was out of the jail, the Magician changed himself back to the size he had been.

Hector, the puppy dog, jumped up and down and barked with joy as he ran alongside his mean master. For, as you know, a puppy dog is always faithful to his master no matter how badly that master may treat him.

"Just you wait, Hector puppy dog!" the Magician said as he winked his eye slyly, "As soon as I get home, I will make a lot of goodies which we will take to the Hooligooly's house. Raggedy Ann, Raggedy Andy, the Hooligoolys and that Policeman fellow will eat them and they will all turn into strange animals. Then you can have fun chasing them through the woods!" And the mean creature chuckled as though he had thought of something real nice to do.

All the way home he laughed and talked to himself as he planned to change Raggedy Ann into a little white bunny and Raggedy Andy into a little black bunny and the Hooligoolys into two squealy pigs.

He would change the Policeman into a fat hoppy toad so that Hector would be sure to catch him.

And, so, the Magician and Hector, the puppy dog, went merrily along thinking of the fun they were going to have when suddenly they arrived at home.

The mean Magician went right to work on his wicked plans while Hector stood by and watched his every move.

WORTH
GRUELLE

Chapter Four

OF COURSE, Raggedy Ann and Andy and the Nice Fat Policeman and the Hooligoolys did not think for one minute that the Mean Magician could get out of the cell in the Policeman's house.

They were all sitting comfortably in the living room at the Hooligoolys telling stories. Each one was to tell a story and they were having just the nicest time ever.

Raggedy Ann turned to Harry Hooligooly and said, "Will you, please, tell the first story since you are our good host?"

"Well, let's see!" Harry Hooligooly mused, "I know so many stories, I do not know which one to tell.

"Tell the one about the Wild Gazook!" Mrs. Hooligooly suggested.

"All right!" Harry laughed.

"Just about a mile from here in the thickest part of the Deep, Deep Woods, there is a queer little house. It is built of stones and sticks and is plastered all over with mud. It has been standing for such a long time that the mud has grown as hard as concrete.

"Whenever we passed this queer little house, we always wondered who lived there, but we could never see anyone about. We knew there must be someone inside, for nearly always smoke would be coming out of the crooked little chimney.

"One day Eddie Elf and I went to the grocery store. As we passed the queer little house on our way to the store, Eddie Elf stopped suddenly and said to me, 'Harry Hooligooly, we have never seen who lives in this funny little house! Let's knock on the door and maybe whoever lives here will come out!'

"I told Eddie Elf that I thought we had better run along to the grocery store first.

" 'You must be afraid!' he replied.

"Indeed I was not afraid. Harry Hooligooly laughed, but I knew some strange person must live there.

"Well, Eddie walked to the front door and knocked.

" 'Who's knocking at my door?' cried a very gruff voice from inside.

" 'Please sir, it's Eddie Elf!' replied Eddie with a little tremor in his voice.

"The door opened quickly and a hand reached out and dragged Eddie Elf into the house.

" 'Dear me!' I said to myself, 'Eddie Elf is surely in trouble now but I will have to try to help him.' So, I walked to the door and knocked.

" 'Who's knocking at my door?' the gruff voice asked again.

" 'It's Harry Hooligooly!' I called loudly so that whoever it was, he would not think I was frightened, 'and I came to get Eddie Elf.'

" 'Ha!' the gruff voice roared, 'Don't you know that I am the Wild Gazook and that I shall make soup out of Eddie Elf?'

" 'You just better send Eddie Elf out here right away or you'll be sorry!' I replied.

" 'Oh, ho!' the gruff voice seemed to roar, 'I guess you don't know how wild a Wild Gazook can be. You had better run along home before I capture you, too!'

"This almost frightened me, for I had never seen a Wild Gazook. But I could not go away and leave Eddie Elf to be made into soup. Think how sad that would have made his nice mama.

"There at my feet on the ground was a large stone and almost without thinking, I picked it up and went to the door and knocked real loudly.

" 'Do you hear that?' I called to the Wild Gazook. 'Well, I tapped the door with my little finger! If I should hit it with my fist, I would break it right in. Then I would give you a thump!'

"There was no answer. Everything was very quiet and my knees shook as I thought the Wild Gazook was about to jump out at me.

"Then I heard the Wild Gazook say to himself, 'My goodness! if he can make so much noise with his little finger, he must be very strong. I think I will put Eddie Elf outside for fear this Hooligooly will give me a thump!'

"Next thing I knew, the door flew open and Eddie Elf came bounding out.

" 'Please do not come in and thump me for it would hurt terribly!' the Wild Gazook was saying from the other side of the door and in a voice not nearly so gruff as before.

" 'Well, I shall not thump you this time, but if I ever hear

of you capturing anyone again, you can be sure that I will hurry over here and give it to you!'

"Eddie Elf and I were so frightened we could hardly walk away but we got over it quickly and were soon running as fast as our legs would take us on the way home and we did not get to the grocery store at all.

"And that is the story of how I rescued Eddie Elf from the clutches of the Wild Gazook."

Raggedy Ann and Andy and the Nice Fat Policeman laughed and laughed at the smart way Harry Hooligooly had fooled the Wild Gazook.

"That is always the way!" Raggedy Ann said, "we are often afraid of things, but if we are brave, the things that

cause us fear usually turn out to be quite harmless and afterwards we laugh at ourselves for being frightened."

When Harry Hooligooly finished his story, Mrs. Hooligooly went to the kitchen and brought a nice plate of cookies and a pitcher of pink lemonade which was welcomed by all.

After they had refreshed themselves, The Nice Policeman turned to Raggedy Ann and said, "Now, Raggedy Ann it is your turn to tell us a story!"

"I will tell you a story!" Raggedy Ann said, "But I will have to make it up as I go along!"

This pleased everyone, for they knew Raggedy Ann had a lovely candy heart and she would be sure to tell a pleasing story.

Raggedy Ann was just ready to begin telling her story when there came a very loud knock at the back door.

"Wait just a moment before you start the story please, Raggedy Ann!" Mrs. Hooligooly asked as she went to the door.

The others laughed and talked while they waited, and, after ten minutes when Mrs. Hooligooly did not return, Harry Hooligooly said, "Excuse me, please, I will go and see what is keeping Henrietta Hooligooly."

The others kept on chatting until another ten minutes had gone by and neither Mr. or Mrs. Hooligooly had come back.

"Excuse me, boys!" Raggedy Ann said, "I will run and see what is keeping the Hooligoolys!"

Raggedy Andy and the Nice Fat Policeman talked and laughed for ten minutes and when Raggedy Ann did not return, Raggedy Andy excused himself and went to see what the trouble could be.

This left the Nice Policeman all alone. He could not very well talk and laugh with himself so he ate a few cream puffs and drank a glass of pink lemonade.

At the end of ten minutes the Nice Fat Policeman said, "Excuse me, I will run out and see what has become of all the others!" When he saw there was no one to talk to, his face turned red and he hurried out of the room.

The Policeman could see no one in the kitchen and he kept on out the back door. In the yard he found signs of scuffling and he knew in a moment that something had happened.

"Yes, sir!" the Nice Fat Policeman said to himself, "I see marks of a tussle here at the kitchen door. I'll bet a cookie the person who knocked at the door grabbed my

friends and scuffled with them. I must go and find them!"

The kind hearted Policeman pulled his detective book from his pocket and read it carefully. Then after a minute or two, he took off his coat, turned it inside out and put on the false whiskers which he always carried in his pocket. Then, as he was completely disguised, he followed the footprints which led through the woods.

On and on went the Policeman following the well marked footprints until they ended suddenly right at the front door of the mean Magician's house.

"Just as I thought!" exclaimed the Nice Fat Policeman, "It's that mean old Magician again!"

The Policeman stood there and listened and listened until his ears turned red but not a sound could he hear coming from inside the house.

Although he felt it was a rude thing to do, the Policeman went around peeping in at all the windows, but he could see nothing for all the curtains had been pulled down.

"Hmmm!" the Nice Fat Policeman mused as he went around to the back porch and sat down to think. "I know they are all inside this house and I must find a way to rescue them!"

Just then the back door was opened very quietly without the Policeman even noticing and the Magician threw a bucket of water all over him.

"Ha, ha, ha!" the Magician laughed as he shut the door and locked it. "Now, perhaps you will not come snooping around here, Mister Tramp!"

The Nice Policeman had disguised himself so well that the Magician did not recognize him at all.

The Policeman shook the water from his clothes as best he could and then walked around and knocked at the front door.

The mean Magician opened the door a tiny crack and asked, "What do you want, tramp, snooping around my house this way?"

"Shhh!" the Policeman whispered, "Are you all alone?"

"No!" the Magician whispered in reply, "I have four

captives in here locked in the flour bin! Why do you ask?"

"Because," the Nice Fat Policeman in disguise replied, speaking as gruffly as he could, "The policeman will be here in a minute to arrest you!"

At this the Magician quickly closed the door with a bang and, as the disguised Policeman jumped back his false whiskers were caught in the door.

"Ah, ha!" shrieked the Magician when he saw the whiskers come off. "I see who it is now! You just better run along home for I shall not let you in nor will I let my captives out!"

The Nice Fat Policeman, feeling very sad and with tears in his eyes, walked slowly away through the woods.

As the Policeman dragged along thinking his hardest to find a way to rescue his friends, he came upon a funny looking little house not far from the path he was following.

It was a little round house made of sticks and stones and covered with mud. The sun had baked the mud until it was hard as stone.

Chapter Five

"WELL!" the Policeman said to himself, "This looks like the home of the Wild Gazook that Harry Hooligooly told us about in his story!"

The Policeman remembered how Harry Hooligooly had fooled the Gazook by knocking on the door with a large stone and he decided to do the same thing.

Bang! Bang! Bang! went the stone against the door and from inside came a quivering voice, "Who is k-k-knocking at m-m-my d-d-door?"

The Policeman was pleased to find his little trick had worked so well and when he also heard the Wild Gazook's teeth chattering, he said, "Aha! I am knocking with my little finger, that's what. If I should knock with my fist, I would surely break the door down!"

"My goodness! You must be very strong!" the Wild Gazook was saying. "Do you wish me to open the door?"

"Indeed I do!" the Policeman replied.

So the Wild Gazook opened the door and the Policeman went inside.

"Now!" the Policeman said, pretending to be very angry, "Tell me whether you have any magical charms around here.

The Gazook, still trembling, walked over to a little cupboard and took up a small bottle which he handed to the Policeman and said, "This will make red whiskers grow on anyone in two minutes!"

"That is great!" thought the Policeman, "Now I can disguise myself so that the mean Magician will never know me!"

The Policeman tried the magical contents of the bottle and, sure enough, long red whiskers appeared on his chin. Then, he turned his coat inside out again and hurried to the home of the Magician and knocked at the door.

"Ho, ho!" the Magician cried, "It's the Policeman again with false red whiskers!"

"Just you feel them and see if they are false!" said the Policeman sticking out his chin.

At this, the Magician gave the Policeman's whiskers a very hard yank, thinking they were false and would come off. Instead the jerk was so hard, the Policeman was yanked right out of his coat which was turned right side out again so that the shiny badge showed and the Magician knew it was, sure enough, the Policeman.

"Ha, ha!" the Magician laughed in a loud ill-mannered way as he went in and slammed the door, "You are just silly if you think you can fool me with your disguises!"

"Are Raggedy Ann and Raggedy Andy and the Hooligoolys still locked up in the flour bin?" the Policeman called after the Magician.

"Yes, they are!" the Magician replied, "And I shall keep them there, too, for I have taken the Magic Burning Stick from Harry Hooligooly's house and I know if I let them go, they will take the Stick away from me again!"

The Policeman was trying his best to think of some way to fool the Magician.

He took the red whisker medicine which the Wild Gazook had given him from his pocket and as he did so, an idea came to him.

"Ha, ha, ha!" the Policeman laughed as he held the bottle near the crack in the door, "I'll bet you would like to have this magic stuff, Mister Magician!"

The Magician reached out and grabbed the bottle, then slammed the door and chuckled at the way he had fooled the Policeman.

"What is this silly stuff?" the Magician wanted to know.

"I shall not tell you!" the Policeman answered, "But, if you put any of it on your chin, I shall surely arrest you!"

"You couldn't arrest a flea!" spoofed the Magician. And to show that he would pay no attention to the Policeman's threats, the Magician promptly rubbed the magic medicine on his chin, opened the door and threw out the empty bottle.

"Dear me!" the Magician cried as he noticed the long

red whiskers dangling from his chin, "Now I know what your magic medicine does!"

Just then a puff of wind blew the Magician's long red whiskers out the crack of the door, and before he could pull them in, the Nice Fat Policeman caught hold of them and held on.

The wicked Magician howled and squealed and the Policeman pulled and tugged until the Magician came howling out onto the porch. The Policeman held firmly to the whiskers and started running and the Magician could do nothing but follow along howling every step of the way.

The Policeman never even slowed down until he had taken the Magician to the jail and locked him securely in a cell.

The Policeman was thinking only of getting back to release his friends from the flour bin, so, he hurried back and left the Magician still howling.

It took the Policeman less than a minute to find the flour bin and let the Raggedys and the Hooligoolys out. They all searched for the Magic Burning Stick and, after they had found it, all went merrily singing back to the Hooligooly's house where they had ice cream and cake and celebrated the happy ending to an exciting adventure.

When things had become quiet once more, Raggedy Ann turned to the Nice Fat Policeman and said, "Please, Mister Policeman, tell us how you managed to rescue us all by yourself!"

"It was all through the magic of the Wild Gazook!" the Fat Policeman said.

And he told how the Wild Gazook had given him the bottle of medicine that grew whiskers by magic.

My! how Raggedy Ann and her friends laughed at this.

"But," Raggedy Ann said, "If the mean Magician escaped from your jail before, why can't he do it again?"

"I never thought of that!" the Fat Policeman said with a worried look, "I shall run home and see about it."

The Policeman ran home as fast as he could and he got there just in time, I can tell you.

As he entered the door to the jail, the little puppy dog ran out.

"Whose puppy dog is that?" the Policeman asked.

"He belongs to me!" the Magician said. "I think I have a right to own a puppy dog if I want to, haven't I?"

"Of course you have, silly!" the Policeman replied, "But I have not arrested the puppy dog, have I? Of course not! Then, the puppy dog has no reason to be in my jail!"

"Oh dear!" the Magician cried, forgetting that he was talking out loud, "If Hector, the puppy dog, is kept out, how can he bring me my magic medicine that will make me shrink small enough to get through these bars!"

"Aha! Mister Magician!" the Policeman cried, "Now I know how you escaped the other time. But this time, I shall see that the magic medicine that makes you shrink does not reach you!"

Then the Policeman sat on the floor behind the door and closed the door all but a crack just large enough to let the puppy dog in. Very soon the puppy dog came bounding in with the bottle of magic shrink medicine held in his teeth and the Policeman just reached out and took the bottle.

"Now, sir, you run home!" the Policeman commanded the puppy dog.

"Here Hector!" the Magician called, "Here Hector! Here!" But the puppy dog ran home as fast as he could and the Policeman laughed, for he would not have hurt the little dog for anything in the world.

The Policeman took the bottle and poured some of the magic shrink medicine on each of the iron bars of the prison cell and they shrunk so close together, the Magician knew that now he would not be able to get out between them.

The Policeman then locked the front door of the jail so the puppy dog could not get in and ran laughing to the Hooligoolys to tell his friends they had nothing more to fear from the wicked Magician.

Raggedy Ann heard the Nice Fat Policeman coming and she ran to the door to meet him. "Is the Magician still locked up in the cell at your police station?" she asked him.

"You bet he is, Raggedy Ann, and I am going to see he stays there!" the Policeman replied as he went into the living room to join the Hooligoolys and Raggedy Andy.

"We were afraid he might have escaped!" Raggedy Andy said with a broad smile.

"That is just great!" Mrs. Hooligooly remarked. "Let us go down and thank the Wild Gazook for helping us!"

This suggestion pleased everyone and without delay they started for the home of the Wild Gazook.

They were tripping merrily along when they came to a fallen tree which they had to climb over and it was right

here that the Policeman met with unusual misfortune. As he started to climb over the fallen tree after helping Raggedy Ann and Mrs. Hooligooly over, his coat caught on a broken limb. Harry Hooligooly helped the Policeman get loose and in jumping down, the Policeman slipped and fell. He did not hurt himself one bit but a strange look came over his kindly face and he began to shrink and wither away.

After the Nice Fat Policeman had poured the magic shrink medicine on the iron bars in the jail, he had slipped the bottle in his pocket. Now the bottle had broken and the medicine had run out all over him.

He was now a very strange looking person and there

seemed to be an excellent reason for him crying as he did.

Raggedy Ann tried to wipe the medicine from the Policeman with her pocket hanky, but it had already done its magical work. So they all gathered around the shrunken little Policeman and felt very sad.

"Dear me!" Raggedy Ann cried when she saw how skinny the Nice Fat Policeman had become, "What shall we do?"

None of them could think of anything to do right then so they sat down and tried to keep the Nice Policeman from crying so much.

"Oh, I wish the mean old Magician had not sent the puppy dog for the shrink medicine!" the Nice Policeman sobbed, "For then I would not have had the bottle in my pocket and this never would have happened."

Raggedy Ann wiped the Policeman's eyes with her clean white apron and tried to comfort him by saying, "You haven't shrunk at all for the last two minutes. Do you think you can walk?"

Although the Policeman was quite wabbly on his legs, with Raggedy Ann on one side and Raggedy Andy on the other, he was able to walk along slowly and it was but a short time when they came to the house of the Wild Gazook.

Raggedy Ann walked up to the front door and knocked softly with her rag hand and, as the others watched, Raggedy Ann walked inside.

"Gracious me!" Mrs. Hooligooly cried, "The Wild Gazook will capture Raggedy Ann and eat her up!"

"Oh, no!" Raggedy Andy replied, "Raggedy Ann is made of cloth just as I am, and the Wild Gazook will not eat cloth. Only goats eat cloth!"

"Well," the shriveled Policeman said in a weak little voice, "The Wild Gazook looks very much like a Billy goat.

Quick, Raggedy Andy, you and Harry Hooligooly dash around to the back door and knock with a big stone. The Wild Gazook will think you are very strong and will become frightened, then you can rescue Raggedy Ann!"

Raggedy Andy and Harry Hooligooly lost no time in doing this and when the Wild Gazook opened the door, there

sat Raggedy Ann happily drinking an ice cream soda.

"Come in and have an ice cream soda!" the Wild Gazook said, so, Raggedy Andy called the Policeman and Mrs. Hooligooly and they all went into the Gazook's house.

The Wild Gazook had a little soda fountain at one side of his funny little round room and he soon had a glass of ice cream soda for everyone.

"What is the matter with the Policeman?" the Wild

Gazook asked, "When he came here a short time ago he was nice and fat, now he is very thin!"

Raggedy Ann told the Gazook how the Policeman had come to shrink as the result of breaking the bottle of magic medicine and when she finished the story, the Wild Gazook was crying.

"I feel so sorry for the Nice Policeman!" sobbed the Gazook, "And I know how he feels because I, too, am under a magic spell. I am not really a goat. I am this way because a mean magician changed me with his magic."

"Isn't there any way we can help you, Mister Gazook?" the Nice Policeman asked.

"I do not know!" the Wilk Gazook replied, "I have tried all sorts of magic medicines, but none of them seem to help me. I have been like this for a long, long time. But, let me see if some of the magic potions I have here will not help the Nice Policeman."

The Wild Gazook went to a little cupboard and the very first bottle he took down changed the Policeman in three shakes so that he was just as fat and merry as he had been before. The Gazook was so happy over this that he insisted on all sitting down and having another ice cream soda.

While they were enjoying the sodas, Raggedy Ann asked, "Please, Mister Wild Gazook, will you tell us how you came to have the magic worked on you which makes you look like a Billy goat?"

"I shall be glad to tell you," the Wild Gazook answered, "But it is a very, very sad story!"

The policeman got out his hanky, for he was very tenderhearted, and the Wild Gazook went on with his story.

"I lived farther back in the Deep Woods with my Grandma and she was so very nice, I loved her dearly but Granny was so old it was hard for her to do much work.

WORTH GRUELLE

"I cut the wood, built the fire and sometimes cooked the meals. One day, when I was gathering firewood in the Deep Woods not far from our cottage, I cut a limb from a fallen tree. I could see no difference between this and any other piece of firewood, but when I took it home, Grandma knew the moment she saw it that it was the Magic Burning Stick.

"Grandma told me to place the Magic Stick in the fireplace and tell it to burn. And, when I did this the stick blazed and gave out much heat. Then Grandma said, 'Magic Stick, stop burning!' and the blaze went out immediately and the stick was just as it had been before.

"The Magic Burning Stick made things easy for Grandma. When she wanted to cook, she just called on the Magic Stick and it never failed. But one day while I was away, a mean man came to the cottage and took the Magic Stick from Granny and carried Granny away, too. I followed his footprints right to this very house. I rushed in and made for him but before I could catch hold of him, he threw some strange medicine on me and changed me into a Wild Gazook.

"I guess he did not know what he would change me into, for, when he saw me as a Wild Gazook, he seemed frightened and rushed out of the house and I have not seen him since.

"I have always felt so ashamed to think I look like a Billy goat that I hardly ever go outside of this little house."

"But, how do you get things to eat?" Raggedy Andy asked.

The Wild Gazook laughed, "You see those boxes on the shelf? They are filled with food. And they are magic boxes. The minute one gets empty, it fills right up again. I'll show you!"

And the Wild Gazook went to one of the boxes and took out two delicious pies for his new friends.

"I'll bet we know the mean man, who took your Magic Burning Stick!" Raggedy Andy exclaimed. And he told the Wild Gazook about the mean Magician.

"Ha!" the Gazook cried, and he looked very wild indeed, "I will catch that wicked Magician and he will be very sorry for the mean things he has done!"

And the Wild Gazook would have rushed out then, but his friends were not finished eating the pie and the Wild Gazook knew it would be impolite for him to leave, so he sat down and waited patiently until they had finished.

"Mister Wild Gazook!" Raggedy Ann said, "Your story was very sad and we want to help you find your dear Grandma. We will show you were the mean Magician lives but I think it best for him not to see you. If he sees you, he will not tell us what he has done with your Grandma and, if you fight him, we will not be able to find out how to change you from a Wild Gazook to what you were before!"

"Raggedy Ann is right!" the Nice Fat Policeman said, "We will have to go about this carefully!"

"I am very eager to see him and make this mean Magician give back my dear Granny and change me back into the nice boy that I was before he threw that magic medicine on me!" the Wild Gazook said.

"Now, if everyone is ready," the Nice Fat Policeman said, "We will take the Wild Gazook to the police station. He can peep in and see the Magician and hear what we say to him. Then, if the Magician will not tell us what he did with the Wild Gazook's Granny, we will have the Wild Gazook go right into the cell and make the Magician feel sorry."

When they reached the jail, the Nice Policeman, Raggedy Ann, Raggedy Andy and Mr. and Mrs. Hooligooly went inside and closed the door all but for a little crack through which the Wild Gazook peeped.

The Gazook had hardly reached the door when he heard a loud cry from all of the friends that had gone inside. The wicked old Magician had escaped again and Raggedy Ann was doing her best to cheer the sobbing Policeman.

Chapter Six

"OH, DEAR! Oh, dear!" wailed the Policeman, "The iron bars are still very close together just as I left them when I poured the shrink medicine on them. How could that wicked Magician get through such a small space?"

No one seemed to be able to answer this question. It seemed just like a real hard riddle.

"Well, then!" the Policeman continued, "What had we better do? Shall we go to the Magician's house and see if he is there?"

Although no one said anything, they all started on the run to the Magician's house.

The Policeman was in the lead and when he reached the front gate, he waited until the others came up and said, "Now if we all run up to the door, the Magician will hear us and try to do something mean. I think I had better tip-toe up and peep in the window. Then I will come back and tell you what I see!"

Very quietly the Nice Policeman tiptoed to the window. At first, the Policeman thought the Magician was not at home because inside the house it seemed very dark.

Of course, this is true of all magicians' homes. For, you know, if they were light and sunny, a wicked magician would not like it. Just the same as when a person keeps his heart filled with the sunshine of happiness, there is no way for him to do unkind things.

The longer the Policeman looked in the window the better he could see in the dark inside. And, after a while he could just make out the Magician stirring something on a stove, as the Policeman looked through the doorway into the little back room.

The Policeman listened closely and heard the Magician talking. He was saying, "I'll bet the silly, fat policeman will be surprised when he goes to the jail and finds that I have escaped again. If it had not been for my pet poll parrot flying in the window of the jail with my invisible medicine, I probably would never have been able to get out of the prison!" And the Magician chuckled to himself in a very satisfied way.

When he heard this, the Policeman tiptoed quickly to his friends and told them.

"Now we must think of a way to capture this mean creature!" Raggedy Ann said. "The Wild Gazook must find his Grandma, we must get the Magic Burning Stick, and then, we must fix the Magician so that he can never work magic again!"

They were all quietly thinking real hard when Raggedy Andy suggested, "Maybe if we all run up to the Magician's front door and yell like everything, he will be startled at the racket we make and may tip over the magic medicine. Then, if the magic medicine spills all over the Magician, it may change him into some mean little animal and then we can catch him and make him tell."

Everybody got ready and when Raggedy Andy counted one, two, three, all ran shouting towards the Magician's house and stamped their feet and jumped up and down on the front porch.

It worked fine. It almost frightened the Magician out of his shoes. He let out a startled cry and dropped the large spoon with which he was stirring the magic medicine and ran lickety split out the back door and into the deep woods.

"That is enough!" Raggedy Andy called when his friends had jumped up and down and squealed and yelled sixty 'leven times, "Now we will go in and see if he has spilled the magic medicine!"

Into the house they all went, to see that the Magician had left hastily by the back door.

"We must follow and capture him!" the Nice Fat Policeman cried, "Come on!"

All but Raggedy Ann hurried along with the Policeman following the Magician's footprints away through the woods.

Raggedy Ann stayed behind and gathered up a lot of

tiny bottles filled with magic medicine which she put into a little basket and then raced along to join the others.

Raggedy Ann overtook them in a little while. They were all standing around watching the Kind Policeman who was acting very strangely. He was running around in circles and jumping over stones and logs.

"What is the matter?" Raggedy Ann asked as she ran up and caught the Policeman by the arm.

"Let me go!" the Nice Fat Policeman cried, "I've lost

my breath and I'm trying to catch it!" And he struggled so hard that Raggedy Andy and the Wild Gazook and Harry Hooligooly had to help Raggedy Ann hold him.

"How do you expect to catch your breath by running after it?" Raggedy Ann asked the Policeman. "You must sit quietly, then your breath thinks you want to play and it comes up real close and you can catch it easily!"

The Policeman knew Raggedy Ann's advice was always good, so, he sat down at once and began to twiddle his thumbs. In just a few minutes he felt his breath returning and knew he had caught it again. "Now we can go on, Raggedy Ann!" he said, "And the next time I lose my breath, I will know just how to find it!"

They all ran as fast as they could in the direction the Magician had gone.

After a long time of running, the Nice Policeman again lost his breath. He sat down to catch it and the others were glad to rest, too.

They had not been resting three minutes in the little clump of bushes when, the Magician, thinking the others had given up chasing him, came quietly along never thinking the others were anywhere near.

He was grinning at the thought of having run away from Raggedy Ann and the others and that they had to give up the chase.

The Magician stopped just before he came to the clump of bushes where our friends were hiding and took his Book of Magic from his pocket. It was a little green book. And, while it was not as complete as the large red Book of Magic he had at home, it told how to do a lot of magical things.

"Isn't he just the meanest old thing you ever saw?" the Nice Policeman whispered as they watched him studying his Book of Magic and probably planning more mischief.

"Let's get him now!" Raggedy Andy whispered as he and the Nice Fat Policeman, Harry Hooligooly and the

Wild Gazook pounced quickly on the Magician and threw him to the ground. Raggedy Andy hurried to take the little green Book of Magic from the Magician before he could work even one speck of magic.

The boys tied the hands and feet of the mean Magician to be sure that he would not run away again and then Raggedy Ann came over and spoke quietly to him.

"Mister Mean Magician!" Raggedy Ann began, "The Wild Gazook tells us that you went into the house where he lived with his nice Grandma and took their Magic Burning Stick and his Grandma away with you and that you threw some magic medicine on him that changed him to a Wild Gazook. Why did you do that?"

The mean old Magician looked very, very angry and it was a long time before he replied, "I didn't take his Magic Burning Stick and I didn't take away his Grandmother and I didn't change him into a Wild Gazook!"

"Oh; that's the biggest fib I ever heard!" the Wild Gazook cried, "You should be ashamed of yourself!"

"Well, I'm not!" the mean old Magician cried, "Just you let me up before I call a policeman and have you all arrested! That's what!"

"Ha, ha, ha!" Raggedy Andy laughed. "We have a policeman right here helping us hold you! Now what have you to say?"

"Anyway, I didn't do any of the things the Wild Gazook says that I did!" the Magician growled.

"I'll bet a nickel he did!" Harry Hooligooly said, "For he took my Magic Burning Stick!"

"Oh! I did not!" the Magician howled.

"Dear me!" Raggedy Ann said pointing her rag hand at the Magician's nose, "Don't you know it is wrong to tell fibs—very, very wrong? Why, what would your mama say if she knew you told a fib? It would make her feel so sorry, I am sure she would cry! All mamas feel sorry when their children tell fibs. Because when they start telling fibs, the fibs soon grow into naughty lies that cause trouble. You must not tell fibs!"

Tears came into the eyes of the mean old Magician, but he was so angry at the Raggedys and their friends that he said, "Well, I shall not tell any more fibs because I would not like to have my mama feel sorry! I will tell you nothing more! So there!"

This was too much for the Wild Gazook and he started butting the magician around to punish him. Suddenly the Magician jumped up and started running, the strings that tied his hands and feet had broken.

All our friends were so surprised they simply sat and stared at each other.

Chapter Seven

"OH, DEAR!" the Wild Gazook moaned, "Now I will always have to remain a Wild Gazook and I shall never see my dear Granny again!"

The others tried to assure and calm the Wild Gazook

"Just a minute!" Raggedy Ann said. "Please give me that little green Book of Magic, Raggedy Andy!"

Raggedy Andy handed her the book which he had taken from the Magician and Raggedy Ann looked through it.

"There is no use of chasing the Magician when he has such a start. The thing we must try to do is to get the big red Book of Magic away before he reaches home. We have the little green book and if we can get the big red book, the Magician will be unable to work any more of his mean magic."

"Now be very quiet, everyone!" Raggedy Ann continued, "So that I will make no mistake in doing just as the book says. First it says to open both eyes, place the right foot over the left and cross your thumbs. While in this position say, 'Doodledoodle! Chugmug! Wabbledysquack!'

WORTH GRUELLE

and think of the thing you wish to come to you. That will be easy and we shall soon see if the little green book is correct!"

"Does it say how long we will have to wait, Raggedy Ann?" the Nice Fat Policeman asked.

"It doesn't say!" Raggedy Ann replied, "But I do not think it will take long!"

After they had waited five minutes and nothing had happened, Raggedy Andy suggested, "Maybe something is on top of the large red Book of Magic and it cannot move!"

"Maybe so!" Raggedy Ann agreed, "I will do it all over again and wish for the large red Book of Magic to bring anything which may be holding it right along!"

So, when Raggedy Ann had again finished the directions as given in the little green Book of Magic, there came a crashing and struggling in the bushes and out into the open came the large red Book of Magic while hanging on to it pulling and tugging trying to hold it back was the old Magician.

Raggedy Andy and the Nice Fat Policeman quickly caught the Magician and held him.

Raggedy Ann always felt sorry for anyone no matter how mean he might have been. This was, no doubt, because the heart sewed inside her cotton stuffed body was made of candy and had the words "I Love You" written on it.

Raggedy Ann spoke softly to the old Magician as Andy and the Policeman held him securely. "Now perhaps you will tell us what you did with the Wild Gazook's nice Grandma! You have hidden her somewhere!"

The old Magician seemed to be thinking hard. "Well, Raggedy Ann!" he said, "Since you now have my little green book and my big red book so that I cannot work any more magic, I may as well tell you. You will find the Wild Gazook's nice Grandma in my house!"

"But, we have looked all through your house!" Raggedy Ann said. "Surely you must be mistaken!"

"No siree!" the Magician replied, "I changed her with my magic into a copper coffee pot so that no one would ever find her!"

"Ha, ha, ha!" Harry Hooligooly laughed, "He's telling another fib, I'll bet. How could he change a nice Grandma into a coffee pot?"

"But he changed the Wild Gazook into a Wild Gazook!" Raggedy Andy said, "And, if he could do that, why couldn't he change a nice Grandma into a coffee pot?"

"Let us take the Magician to his house and find out!" suggested the Nice Policeman as he and Andy started off with the old Magician and the others followed right along.

Sure enough, when they reached the home of the Magician, there was the copper coffee pot and with the aid of the large red Book of Magic, Raggedy Ann quickly changed the coffee pot back into the Wild Gazook's Grandma. She was a very nice old lady and her new friends loved her immediately. But the nice Grandma was afraid of the Wild Gazook until Raggedy Ann with the help of the red Book of Magic changed him back to what he had been before. And all were pleased to see a very handsome little boy.

Grandma threw her arms around her little grandson and hugged him tightly. "Now," she said, "You must all come to our house and bring the Magician along, for there are a great many things we must talk over!"

So, with the mean old Magician in the center of them, all our friends went to the cunning little home of Grandma Gazook.

Raggedy Ann placed a chair in the center of Grandma

Gazook's living room and told the Magician to sit there and be very quiet. Then all our friends drew up chairs and sat in a circle around the Magician.

All of a sudden the old Magician put his head in the crook of his arm and began to cry.

Raggedy Andy tried to cheer up the old Magician. "Do not weep!" he said, "It will just make your nose redder and redder and redder and redder!"

"I cannot help weeping!" the mean old Magician said,

"When I think how nice all of you are and how mean I have treated you! I took Grandma Gazook's Magic Burning Stick home with me, but, do you know, it disappeared! Then when Harry Hooligooly found it, I took it away from him, too! I feel so sad!"

Raggedy Ann wiped the Magician's tears away and said, "When anyone who has done an unkind act feels sad about it, it shows that he has brushed the clouds away and that the sun is beginning to shine in his heart!"

The old Magician smiled at Raggedy Ann and her friends. "I feel ever and ever so much happier than I have felt in a long, long time and I want you all to forgive me, if you can, for the unkind things I have done to you!"

"It makes a lot of difference when everyone is kind and friendly!" Raggedy Ann said with a smile.

"I shall never be a Magician again!" the old Magician remarked, "For, I was really very unhappy when I was doing things with magic."

"And do you know why, Mister Magician?" Raggedy Ann asked and without waiting for an answer went on, "It was because all the magical things you did were selfish, unkind things! One can never expect to be happy in doing mean things to others!"

"Will you let me take the little green Book of Magic, Raggedy Ann?" the Magician asked.

"I will trust the old Magician!" Raggedy Ann thought as she handed him the little green Book of Magic.

The old Magician took the little green book and said a very magical word and at once there was a knock on the door of Grandma Gazook's house.

The old Magician smiled as Grandma Gazook went to the door.

And, when she opened it, what do you suppose? Why! the Magic Burning Stick came bumping in and rolled right in front of Harry Hooligooly.

"It's my Magic Burning Stick!" Harry cried.

"It really belongs to Grandma Gazook!" the Magician said.

"So it does!" Harry and Mrs. Hooligooly both agreed, "It is yours Grandma Gazook!"

Grandma Gazook was happy to have the Magic Stick back once more. "Now!" she said with a broad smile, "Since the Burning Stick is mine again, I shall ask Harry and Mrs. Hooligooly to live here with me so they may share in the goodies that the Magic Stick will help me to make!"

And to show everyone just how nicely the Burning

Stick worked, Grandma Gazook took them all to her kitchen, where, in a very short time she was cooking golden brown doughnuts with holes in them just the right size. Then Grandma sprinkled lots of powdered sugar over them and everybody ate just as many as he wished.

The old Magician handed the little green Book of Magic back to Raggedy Ann after he had used it to return the Magic Stick to Grandma Gazook. "Raggedy Ann!" the Magician said, "You may keep the little green book and the large red one, too!" And with these words the voice of the old Magician broke and tears came to his eyes.

"Please do not cry!" the Nice Fat Policeman said. "We all feel badly!" And he wiped a tear from his eyes.

"And to think!" the Policeman continued, "The Magician used to be so mean and selfish, I had to arrest him once! It was the only time I ever arrested anyone! That is the hard part of being a policeman that's what!"

At this, the Magician stood up with a look of surprise on his face, "Oh! I had forgotten!" he cried as he held on to the back of his chair, "I changed the nice fat man into a policeman a long, long time ago. Don't you remember?" he asked the Policeman.

"Not even a speck!" the Nice Policeman replied, "Are you sure?"

"I cannot remember what you were before I changed you into a Nice Fat Policeman, but you were something, that is certain!"

"Then let's change him back!" Raggedy Andy said, "Raggedy Ann can do it with the large red Book of Magic, I am sure!"

Raggedy Ann put the large red Book of Magic on the table and found the place where directions were given to fit the policeman's case.

"Wait!" the Nice Policeman suddenly cried, "Suppose the Magician changed me from a fat pig into a fat policeman! I would not care to be changed back into a fat pig!"

"That is true!" Harry Hooligooly said, "No one wants to be a pig, even though he might make a pig of himself sometimes! Do not change the Nice Policeman back into a pig!"

Raggedy Ann laughed a soft cottony laugh, "Don't you believe it!" she said. "The Magician always made things worse with his magic when he was so mean, so I am sure the Nice Fat Policeman must have been something even nicer than he is now!"

The Nice Fat Policeman was doubtful, but Raggedy Andy said, "Even if you are changed, Raggedy Ann can change you back into the Nice Fat Policeman again, if you are not satisfied!"

"All right then, go ahead!" the Nice Policeman said as he stood up bravely and Raggedy Ann read the magic words from the book.

All were surprised to see the Nice Fat Policeman slowly change as they watched, into a very happy looking young man.

"There! You see!" Raggedy Ann laughed.

Grandma Gazook gave a glad cry and threw her arms around the young man. "It's Grandpa Gazook, only he is as young as when he disappeared a long time ago."

So in order to make everything just right, Raggedy Ann soon changed Grandma Gazook back to the beautiful young lady she had been at the time of her wedding and everyone caught the hands of young Grandpa and Grandma Gazook and danced around the living room. And the old Magician was as happy as the others.

"There is no telling how much unhappiness the old Magician caused when he was mean and selfish!" Raggedy Ann said. Then, turning to the old Magician she said, "Try to remember any others you might have worked the magic on and made unhappy! If we can find them, we will change them into what they were before!"

The old Magician tried and tried to think, but he finally shook his head. "There must have been many others, Raggedy Ann!" he replied, "I cannot think of them, though! You see when I stopped being a mean old Magician a little while ago, I suppose I forgot the mean things I did!"

"That is quite possible!" Raggedy Ann laughed. "We will try another way! What ever became of little Georgie Gazook's daddy and mama?" she asked Grandma Gazook.

"Yes! Where are they?" Grandpa Gazook asked, "I was a fat policeman so long, I forgot all about them!"

"Perhaps if Raggedy Ann would change the old Magician into what he was before he became a Magician, he would be able to tell us!" Raggedy Andy suggested.

"That is a good idea!" Raggedy Ann cried. "Shall I do it?" she asked the old Magician.

"Yes, indeed, Raggedy Ann!" he replied. "For I do not want to be a Magician any more!" And he stood beside Raggedy Ann while she read the words from the large red Book of Magic.

"My gracious!" Grandma Gazook cried when she saw the change in the Magician, "If he isn't Mr. Grote, the grocer!"

"Yes!" Mr. Grote, who was the old Magician said, "I am your old grocer, but once when I was weighing out sugar, I took out a spoonful and cheated a customer. After that I did it every time I weighed anything for a customer and finally I just turned into a very mean person. Then, I found the books of Magic and became a mean old Magician. Thank you, Raggedy Ann, for changing me back into Mr. Grote! Now I shall return to my grocery store and repay everything I have cheated people out of! If you will come with me, you will see!"

All went along with Mr. Grote to his store and he told all his new friends to help themselves to candy and cookies and anything they wished. And everyone had a lot of fun picking out the nice things they wanted.

As people came into the grocery store to buy things, they would say, "Why, Mr. Grote! Where have you been for such a long, long time?"

Mr. Grote would laugh and reply, "I have been shut up in a very dark house, Mrs. Clinkie!" Meaning, of course, that he had shut himself up within a wall of selfishness. Then he would laugh again and push the money back to the customer saying, "Keep your money, Mr. Jing! I shall never charge for groceries again! Everything, from now on, will be free to all my good friends in the Deep, Deep Woods!"

Raggedy Andy drew Raggedy Ann aside and whispered to her and a broad grin could be seen spreading over their rag faces as they took the large red Book of Magic and

went into the back part of the grocery store together.

"Just having a grocery store isn't enough!" Raggedy Andy said to Raggedy Ann.

"Indeed it isn't!" Raggedy Ann replied as she opened the large red Book of Magic. "We must give him a meat market, too!"

"And a clothing store!" Raggedy Andy added.

"Yes, and a dress and hat store!" Raggedy Ann laughed. "We must think of everything while we have the magic books, Raggedy Andy!"

"Then we must give him a toy store and a book store and an ice cream and soda water department!" Raggedy Andy laughed.

"And we will put in a bakery just for good measure!" Raggedy Ann suggested. Then she said the magic words that were written in the red Book of Magic and at once everything she and Raggedy Andy had mentioned was added to the grocery store belonging to Mr. Grote.

"My gracious!" Mr. Grote cried when he saw the new store join on to the old grocery store, "Someone must be working a lot of magic around here!" When Mr. Grote saw the broad smiles on the faces of Raggedy Ann and Raggedy Andy, he knew they had been working this magic. "Well, you two nice Raggedys, just you come here and tell me what I am to do with all these stores?" And he laughed real happily. "I can never take care of all this!"

"If you do not charge for anything," Raggedy Ann said, "there is no reason why people cannot wait upon themselves!"

"We will help you, Mr. Grote!" Grandma and Grandpa and Georgie Gazook cried.

"And so will we!" Harry and Mrs. Hooligooly both added.

"And we will all live here together and be just the nicest kind of friends!" Mr. Grote laughed.

While all the others walked around through the new stores looking at the lovely things, Raggedy Ann and Raggedy Andy sat and thought many happy thoughts in their cotton stuffed heads.

After several minutes of thinking Raggedy Andy spoke. "Oh, Raggedy Ann!" he said, "Will you let me use the red Book of Magic?"

"Why certainly, Raggedy Andy!" Raggedy Ann replied as she handed the book to him.

Raggedy Andy looked through the book until he found the magic words to use and then he said them very softly.

"I'll bet a nickel Raggedy Andy is doing something real nice!" Raggedy Ann thought. And Raggedy Ann was quite right, for, just at that moment glad cries came from the clothing store, where the others were, and Mr. Grote came running out.

"Oh, Raggedy Ann! Oh, Raggedy Andy!" he called. "Where are you?"

"Here we are!" Raggedy Ann replied from her seat on a box of apples. "What has happened, Mr. Grote?"

"Ha, ha, ha! You grand old Raggedys!" he laughed as

he caught Raggedy Ann's arm. "You know very well, for it must have been one of you who worked the magic that brought so much happiness to Mr. and Mrs. Hooligooly! Only, you must know, the Hooligoolys have disappeared and you will never see them again!"

"Oh dear!" Raggedy Ann cried, "I am so sorry! What could have happened?"

Mr. Grote, who used to be the mean old Magician, did not answer. He led the Raggedys into the store where Grandma and Grandpa and Georgie Gazook all stood with their arms around a strange pretty lady and a fine looking young man.

"Here is my mama and here is my daddy!" Georgie Gazook cried. "And all the time, we did not know who they were!"

"Why, who were they?" Raggedy Ann asked in surprise.

"Don't you know?" Raggedy Andy giggled as he put his rag arm around Raggedy Ann and gave her a soft cottony squeeze. "They were the Hooligoolys and that was why I borrowed the large red Book of Magic!"

"I do not believe you have forgotten a single thing to make our happiness complete!" Grandma Gazook said. "We love you both and thank you for all the nice things you have done for us!"

"We are very, very glad that you all love us!" Raggedy Ann replied. "That makes Raggedy Andy and me very happy, for there is nothing that brings such happiness as loving friendship. But, there is one thing we forgot. Raggedy Andy and I want you to have the two Books of Magic. Then you can always wish for lovely things to bring comforts to yourselves and your friends and to those in need!"

The Raggedys stayed and visited with their friends for

a long time, but after a while they began to be homesick and spoke of this to Mr. Grote.

Mr. Grote was sorry to think of the Raggedys leaving and so was the whole Gazook family but they all knew it would be selfish to keep the Raggedys with them if the Raggedys really wished to return home.

So Raggedy Ann and Raggedy Andy kissed everyone good bye and Grandma with tears in her eyes read from the red Book of Magic while the Raggedys held their rag hands over their shoe button eyes. As the Raggedys listened to Grandma read the magic charm, they could hear her voice grow fainter and fainter until at last all was quiet. Then the Raggedys took their hands down and their shoe button eyes twinkled with happiness for they were sitting in the nursery, while around them with love shining in their eyes, sat all the other dolls.